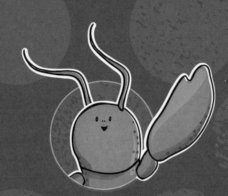

LUCY LOVES SHERMAN'S BEACH

Sky Pony Press
New York

Written by Catherine Bailey and Illustrated by Meg Walters

For my Mimi &
all the fiesty girls
— CB

For my mother Anne
& for Eliza and Andrew
— MW

Sky Pony Press books may be purchased in bulk at special discounts for sales promotion, corporate gifts, fund-raising, or educational purposes. Special editions can also be created to specifications. For details, contact the Special Sales Department, Sky Pony Press, 307 West 36th Street, 11th Floor, New York, NY 10018 or info@skyhorsepublishing.com.

Sky Pony® is a registered trademark of Skyhorse Publishing, Inc.®, a Delaware corporation.

Visit our website at www.skyponypress.com.

10 9 8 7 6 5 4 3 2 1

Manufactured in China, December 2018
This product conforms to CPSIA 2008

Library of Congress Cataloging-in-Publication Data is available on file.

Cover design by Daniel Brount
Cover illustrations by Meg Walters

Print ISBN: 978-1-5107-4358-8
Ebook ISBN: 978-1-5107-4359-5

LUCY LOVED HER BEST FRIEND SHERMAN.

THEY SWAM TOGETHER, BLEW BUBBLES TOGETHER,

AND PLAYED HIDE-AND-GO-SEEK TOGETHER.

UNTIL...

LUCY TUGGED AT THE LINE,

BUT IT WAS TOO TANGLED AND TWISTED.

SHE BEGGED GRAMPS
TO DIVE IN.

"IT'S NOT SAFE. LET'S GO GET HELP."

"I'M NOT LEAVING HIM."

"HE FEELS THREATENED — HE MIGHT PINCH US."

"HE WOULD NEVER!"

"HE'S TOO BIG — WE CAN'T MOVE HIM."

"I HAVE A BUCKET."

LUCY PERSISTED. AS USUAL.

"HE NEEDS ME!"

"PLEASE?"

"WHAT IF AN OCTOPUS COMES BY? OCTOPUSES **EAT** LOBSTERS!"

"I SAID 'PLEASE.'"

"LOOK! THE MARINE CENTER'S RIGHT THERE!"

GRAMPS RESISTED.

BUT ONLY FOR A WHILE.

THIS PROBLEM WAS
BIGGER
THAN SHERMAN!

"WHY HASN'T ANYBODY FIXED THIS?"

SHERMAN SPLASHED.

LUCY GASPED.

SHE HAD TO ACT.

FIRST LUCY HUNG HELPFUL SIGNS.

BUT THE LIFEGUARD MADE HER TAKE THEM DOWN.

AND WHEN SHE TRIED BUILDING A FENCE,
GRAMPS TOOK AWAY HER TOOLS.

"ALRIGHT, LUCY. ENOUGH IS ENOUGH. I'M SORRY BUT THESE FOLKS AREN'T GOING TO LISTEN TO YOU."

"THEY WILL IF YOU GIVE ME BACK MY MEGAPHONE . . ."

GRAMPS SIGHED.

"HONEY, YOU CAN'T KEEP PEOPLE OFF THE BEACH. IT'S OPEN TO THE PUBLIC. BESIDES, HUNDREDS OF FOLKS LOVE THE BEACH, JUST LIKE YOU LOVE SHERMAN."

HUNDREDS?

SUDDENLY LUCY HAD AN IDEA.

SHE STARTED WITH GRAMPS AND NANA.

GRAMPS SHOOK HIS HEAD.

"LUCY, WE CAN'T POSSIBLY ..."

"HERE ARE YOUR RUBBER GLOVES."

THEN THEY BUMPED INTO SOME FRIENDS.

Well, it is a beautiful day to be outside.

This is great exercise!

SURFERS AND SAILORS.

SUNBATHERS AND SWIMMERS.

FAMILIES AND FISHERMEN.

EVERYONE PITCHED IN.

SOON THE SAND WAS SPOTLESS.

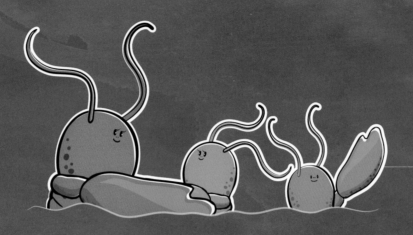

EVEN THE WAVES SPARKLED.

EVERYBODY AGREED. THEIR BEACH WAS BEAUTIFUL,

AND IT WOULD STAY THAT WAY.

AS THE SUN SET, LUCY AND SHERMAN WAVED
GOOD NIGHT TO EACH OTHER.

THEN LUCY HAD ONE MORE IDEA.

REDUCE. REUSE. RECYCLE.

EVERYBODY'S
BEACH

WHEN I SAVED SHERMAN'S BEACH, I LEARNED A LOT ABOUT POLLUTION. YOU MAY KNOW THAT POLLUTION IS ANYTHING THAT MAKES OUR EARTH DIRTY, UNHEALTHY, OR UNSAFE TO USE, BUT DID YOU KNOW THAT MORE THAN 100,000 SEA MAMMALS – AND 1 MILLION SEABIRDS! – ARE KILLED BY POLLUTION EACH YEAR?

CHECK OUT THE FOLLOWING "TRASH TALK" FOR MORE ECO-INFO:

Ecosystem:
A carefully balanced system of living things, such as plants and animals, and non-living things, like the weather and soil, that exist and interact harmoniously together.

Environment:
The area in which someone or something exists, and everything in it. For example your school, from the teachers to the textbooks, is an environment.

Water Pollution:
Trash, harmful chemicals, and other materials that damage bodies of water, likes oceans, lakes, and rivers. These destructive materials, or pollutants, don't stay in one place. They can ride the currents of our seas and oceans around the world.

Land Pollution:
Trash, harmful chemicals, and other materials that damage Earth's soil. A common source of land pollution is litter, which means garbage that is not properly thrown away. The picnickers' wrappers and bottles are examples of litter.

Air Pollution:
Harmful gases that pollute the air, like the exhaust fumes from buses and cars. Walking and biking instead of driving is an easy way to reduce air pollution. When air pollution is really bad, it can be seen. It looks like smoke, and it is called smog.

Light Pollution:
Unnecessary and extended use of artificial lights that disrupts the normal activities of wildlife, like sea turtles who will only lay their eggs on dark beaches.

Conservation:
Keeping the natural environment the way it is and protecting it from pollution. Conservation includes educating others, like when Dr. Bait talked to Lucy.

Biodegradable:
Able to be broken down into something that is safe for the environment.

Waste:
Anything that is thrown away or not used.

Reduce, Reuse, Recycle:
Three environmentally friendly ways to deal with waste. Reduce means to buy less stuff, like getting one polka-dotted bathing suit instead of two! Reuse means finding a new way to use something you have so it doesn't become trash. Recycling means using trash to make entirely new products.

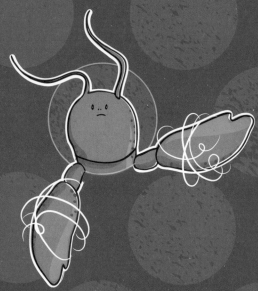

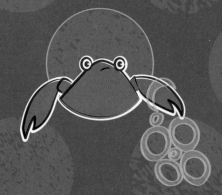